In the dark bedroom of a little boy, the closet door creaked open. The boy snapped awake as a huge, scary monster crept up to his bed and spread its arms wide, preparing to roar! But the boy's scream scared the monster and it staggered back and fell to the floor.

Suddenly, the lights came on and the bedroom wall opened up. The boy turned out to be just a robot and the monster was a trainee. Monster Bile was learning to scare children at Monsters, Inc., the largest scream-processing factory in Monstropolis. Ms. Flint, the scare instructor, turned to the class of trainees. "Can anyone tell me Mr. Bile's big mistake?"

Mr. Bile had left the closet door open. "And leaving the door open is the worst mistake any employee can make because . . ."

"It could let in a child!"

The trainees spun around to see Mr. Waternoose, the crablike, five-eyed president of Monsters, Inc., at the back of the room. "There's nothing more toxic or deadly than a human child. A single touch could kill you!"

Meanwhile, the company's best Scarer, a huge, hairy, blue-spotted monster named James P. Sullivan, or Sulley for short, was walking to work with his friend, Mike Wazowski. Mike was a little green ball of a monster with one enormous eye. Mike wanted to drive his new car, but Sulley disagreed. "Mikey, there's a scream shortage."

You see, monsters captured the screams of children and used them to power their world, but kids weren't as easy to scare as they used to be.

Mike and Sulley arrived at the factory for work. It was a big day for Sulley because he was about to break the all-time scare record. They crossed the lobby to the receptionist, Celia, who was also Mike's girlfriend.

"Oh, Schmoopsie-Poo . . ."

"Googly bear!"

It was Celia's birthday, and Mike was taking her to a fancy sushi restaurant that night to celebrate. "I will see you at quittin' time and not a minute later."

"Okay, sweetheart."

Sulley and Mike crossed to their workstation on the Scare Floor, the busy room where all the scaring in the factory took place.

Mike slipped a card key into a slot and a door emerged from a huge overhead vault and dropped into place in front of them. At the next station, a lizardlike monster named Randall made his preparations. Randall was the company's second best Scarer, but he was determined to take the lead.

Sulley waved to him. "Hey—may the best monster win."

"I plan to."

Red lights lit up above all the doors to show they were active. Mike cheered Sulley on as he opened his door and crossed into a child's room.

"You're the boss, you're the boss, you're the big hairy boss!"

Sullivan kept his lead. "Oh, I'm feeling good today, Mikey!"

"'Atta boy, 'atta boy! Another door coming right up."

Randall's assistant, Fungus, turned to his boss. "You're still behind, Randall."

"Just get me another door!"

Suddenly, an alarm sounded. "2319! We have a 2319!" Another monster, George, had come out of his door with a human sock stuck to his back. "Get it off! Get it off!"

Agents from the Child Detection Agency, or CDA, swarmed onto the Scare Floor. They knocked poor George to the ground, picked off the sock, and blew it up. George was disinfected in a shower and shaved clean.

Mr. Waternoose was not pleased. "An entire Scare Floor out of commission. What else can go wrong?"

Despite the temporary setback, Sulley still had a good day. "Another day like this and that scare record's in the bag!"

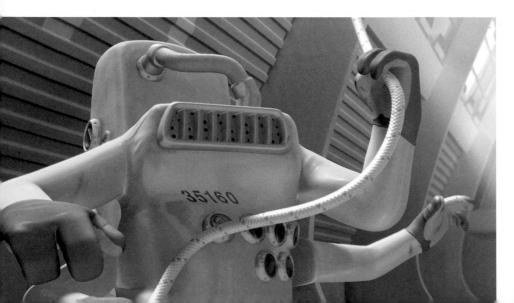

Mike headed out quickly. "Oooh, the love boat is about to set sail."

Just then, Roz, the sluglike dispatcher, stopped him.

"Hello, Wazowski. I'm sure you filed your paperwork correctly. For once."

Mike was caught. He hadn't filed it and Celia was waiting. But Sulley jumped in and offered to file the paperwork for him. "On my desk, Sulley!"

When Sulley returned to the empty Scare Floor, he discovered a lone door that had accidentally been left behind. The door's red light was on. Sulley peered into the child's bedroom. No monsters there. But then he turned around to find a little girl holding his tail!

Quickly he put the girl back in her room and took off. In the locker room he found that the girl was still clinging to his back!

"Kitty!"

Sulley scooped the girl into a duffel bag and ran back to the Scare Floor. But Randall was there, sending the girl's door back to the vault. Sulley couldn't get her back to her room.

Sulley took the duffel bag and rushed to the crowded restaurant where Mike and Celia were dining.

"Get out of here. You're ruining everything!"

"Look in the bag!"

Mike looked, but it was too late. The kid was out of the bag. "Boo!"

"Ahhh! A kid!"

Panicked diners fled the restaurant as CDA agents arrived. Mike and Sulley snatched up the kid and ran. Mike looked back, but the CDA were already taking Celia away. "Michael? Michael!"

"Well, I don't think that date could've gone any worse."

The terrified monsters took the girl back to their
apartment. She ran around happily until she grabbed a one-
eyed teddy bear and Mike objected.

"Hey, hey, that's it. No one touches little Mikey!" And he
grabbed the teddy back.

Her scream made the lights in the apartment surge
brightly. Panicked, Mike ran to the window and pulled the
blinds shut. But as he tried to get the bear back to the girl, he
slipped, flew through the air, and landed in a wastebasket.
Amazingly, her laughter caused all the lights in the whole
building to light up and blow out.

"What was that?"

"I have no idea, but it would be really great if it didn't do it
again."

After a lot of playing, the little girl finally got tired, and Sulley put her to bed in his room. But as Sulley started to leave, she whimpered and pointed to the closet. She showed Sulley a picture she had drawn.

"Hey, that looks like Randall. Randall's your monster. How 'bout I sit here, until you fall asleep?" Sulley comforted her gently until she fell asleep.

Then he returned to the living room. "Hey, Mike—this might sound crazy, but I don't think that kid's dangerous."

Sulley figured the best plan was to get the girl back to her room through her closet door at Monsters, Inc.

The next day, he disguised her in a little monster costume and took her back to the factory.

"Sulley, a mop, a couple of lights, and some chair fabric are not gonna fool anyone. Loch Ness, bigfoot, the abominable snowman. They all got one thing in common, pal . . . banishment! We could be next!"

Of course, they promptly ran into Mr. Waternoose.

"Boo!"

"Ah-ha! James! Is this one yours?"

"Uh, actually . . . that's my . . . uh, cousin's . . . sister's . . . uh, daughter, sir." The guys ducked into the restroom with the girl, and she and Sulley played hide-and-seek. "Where did she go? Did she turn invisible?"

"Boo!"

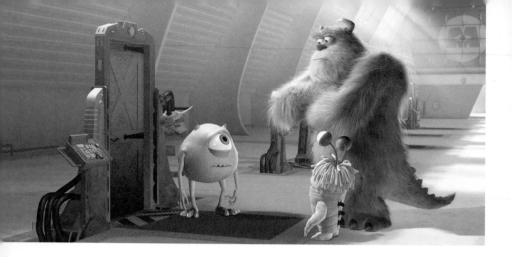

But someone was coming. The girl acted scared, and all three hid in a stall just before Randall and Fungus entered. "What are we going to do about the child?"

"Shhh! You just get the machine up and running, I'll take care of the kid. And when I find whoever let it out . . . they're dead!"

Mike and Sulley hurried the girl to their station on the Scare Floor. Mike swiped a card key and brought a door down from the vault.

"Mike, that's not her door. Her door was white. And it had flowers on it. This isn't Boo's door."

"Boo? What's Boo? Sulley, you're not supposed to name it! Once you name it, you start getting attached to it! Now say good-bye to—Where'd it go? What'd you do with it?"

Sulley scanned the floor for her. "Where is she? Aah! Boo!"

He took off, looking for her. Mike tried to stop him. "Somebody else will find the kid, it'll be their problem, not ours!"

Mike passed Randall in the hall just as Celia approached. "Michael Wazowski! Last night was one of the worst nights of my entire life, bar none!"

"I thought you liked sushi."

"Sushi?! You think this is about sushi?!"

Randall knew that the little girl had appeared at a sushi restaurant and he guessed that Mike was involved. "Where's the kid?"

"You're not pinning this on me!"

Randall told Mike the Scare Floor was about to empty out for lunch and that Boo's door would be in his station. "You have until then to put the kid back."

Meanwhile, Sulley searched everywhere for Boo. He finally spotted her climbing into a garbage can. "No!"

But CDA agents stopped to get Sulley's autograph just as some workers appeared and wheeled off the can. Sulley ran up in time to see the workers tip the can down the trash chute, not knowing that Boo had already climbed out and toddled off. He raced down to the basement, where the trash was processed, and watched horrified as it was smashed into a cube by a giant compactor.

Mike caught up to Sulley crying and cradling the garbage cube in his arms. "I can still hear her little voice."

"Mike Wazowski!" Boo was with a group of day-care children and their teacher. "Kitty!"

"Boo!" The delighted Sulley picked Boo up and hugged her tightly.

"Okay, Sulley. That's enough. Let's go . . ."

On the deserted Scare Floor, Mike spotted Boo's door set up in Randall's station.

"There it is! Just like Randall said!"

"Mike, what are you thinking? We can't trust Randall. He's after Boo."

"You want me to prove everything's on the up-and-up? Fine." Mike marched into Boo's room and began bouncing on her bed. Suddenly, a large box flew up from behind the bed and trapped him. After a moment, Randall peeked out of Boo's room. Sulley comforted Boo, and they hid as Randall loaded the box containing Mike on a cart and rolled it away.

Sulley and Boo followed Randall. They caught up with him just as he was strapping Mike into a giant machine, while Fungus tinkered with the controls. "I'm about to revolutionize the scaring industry. First, I need to know where the kid is. And you're gonna tell me. Say hello to the Scream Extractor."

A huge vacuumlike device descended from the ceiling toward Mike's face. "No! Come on, hey! Randall! Help! Help! Help!"

Sulley pulled the machine's plug. Randall went to investigate, and Sulley quickly freed Mike and snatched up Fungus. Randall returned to find Fungus in the Scream Extractor.

"What happened? Where's Wazowski?"

Sulley decided to go to Mr. Waternoose about the problem. They found him in the training room with a class of trainees. "James! Perfect timing!" Before Sulley could protest, Mr. Waternoose ushered him into the fake bedroom while Mike held Boo. "C'mon, c'mon! What are you waiting for? Roar!"

Boo watched horrified as Sulley was forced to scare the robot child. Boo began to cry and Sulley realized that Boo was truly scared. "Boo, it's me. No, no, no, no. It's okay. I was just . . . Oh, no, don't be scared."

Just then, the hood of Boo's costume slipped off. "The child!"

Still scared, Boo ran from Sulley right into Mr. Waternoose's arms. "I'm sorry you boys got mixed up in this. But now we can set everything straight again. For the good of the company."

Mr. Waternoose brought Mike and Sulley to an active door.
"Uh, sir, that's not her door."

"I know, I know . . . It's yours." And he shoved Mike and
Sulley through the door and slammed it shut behind them.

The two friends found themselves in a snowstorm in the
Himalayas. "We're in the human world! Oh, what a great idea
going to your old pal Waternoose! Too bad he was in on the
whole thing!"

Sulley tried desperately to reopen the door, but it was no
use. They were stuck. Suddenly, the Yeti, a huge, hairy
monster, appeared.

"I understand. It ain't easy being
banished."

The Yeti invited the two distressed
monsters back to his cave.

The Yeti shared his food, talked about his life, and mentioned a village at the bottom of the mountain. As soon as Sulley heard this, he began frantically building a makeshift sled out of the poor Yeti's belongings. Mike was furious. "What about us?! Ever since that kid came in, you've ignored everything I've said and now look where we are. We were about to break the record, Sulley!"

"None of that matters now. Boo's in trouble! I think there might be a way to save her."

Mike was not interested in risking his life to help her, so Sulley grabbed a lantern, hopped on the sled, and sped off down the mountain alone.

Sulley found an active closet door in the village and crossed back into Monsters, Inc. He burst onto the Scare Floor and raced for Randall's secret lab. "Boo!"

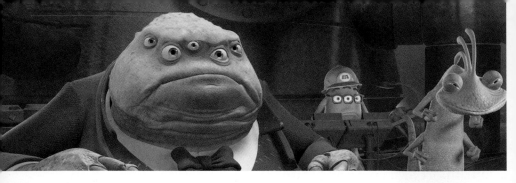

Boo was strapped in the chair, the Scream Extractor inches from her face, as Waternoose and Randall looked on. Sulley charged in like a bull and smashed the machine out of Boo's path. He grabbed Boo and they took off.

"Stop him! Don't let them get away!"

Suddenly, Mike showed up and tried to apologize. Sulley just dragged him along, with Randall chasing after them. They ran to the Scare Floor, and Sulley grabbed onto a door on its way back to the door vault. Sulley, Mike, and Boo clung to the door as it sailed through the enormous vault on a conveyor belt, surrounded by doors as far as the eye could see. Just then, they spotted Randall riding on another door straight toward them.

Sulley shouted. "Make her laugh!"

Mike looked at Boo, then socked himself in the head. The red lights above their door and all the doors in the vault lit up. The trio jumped through the door and found themselves in a house on a beautiful Hawaiian beach. "Why couldn't we get banished here?"

They quickly ran out of the house, into a neighbor's house, and through another door back into the vault. But Randall was still right behind them.

"Hurry up! Keep moving!"

Randall closed in, seized Boo, and disappeared with her into a door. Knowing Sullivan was not far behind, Randall waited, then attacked Sullivan as soon as he appeared in the doorway. "You've been number one for too long, Sullivan! Now your time is up! And don't worry, I'll take good care of the kid!"

Suddenly, Randall's head jerked back. It was Boo, pulling him back! Sulley was saved and was able to get back into the room. "She's not scared of you anymore. Looks like you're out of a job."

Sulley pushed Randall through a door into a run-down trailer in a swamp.

"Mama, 'nother gator got in the house."

"'Nother gator?! Gimme that shovel."

Just then, Boo's door rode by and they jumped on it. But before they could get it open, it lurched off in another direction. "What's happening?"

The door sailed back down toward the Scare Floor where Mr. Waternoose was waiting for them, surrounded by CDA agents.

As the door landed, Mike threw one of Boo's socks at the agents and they all panicked. In the commotion, Mike took off carrying Boo's costume, and the agents followed him. Sulley grabbed Boo's door, and he and Boo ran the other way. Only Mr. Waternoose saw Sulley had Boo, and he chased after them alone.

Sulley ran with Boo to the training room. He quickly put Boo's door in the fake bedroom and hid Boo in the bed to make it look like Boo's room. Mr. Waternoose arrived at the door.

"She's home now. Just leave her alone!"

"I can't do that, she's seen too much! I'll kidnap a thousand children before I let this company die! And I'll silence anyone who gets in my way!"

Suddenly, the lights came on and the walls opened up. Mike was manning the controls, and Waternoose was caught red-handed. As Mike and Sulley watched, CDA agents crossed onto the stage, arrested him, and led him away.

Sulley used a card key to activate Boo's door. She was delighted to see her room again, and showed Sulley around. She looked in her closet.

"Nothing's coming out of your closet to scare you anymore. Right? Yeah. Good-bye, Boo."

"Kitty."

Sulley quietly stepped into the closet and closed the door behind him. The CDA then shredded Boo's door to prevent future monsters from getting into her room. Sulley could never see Boo again.

Thanks to Sulley and Mike's discovery of the superior power of children's laughter, Monsters, Inc. soon switched from screams to giggles. Sulley took over as president and Mike became their best comedian, keeping kids in stitches all day long. But Sulley was sad. He missed Boo. One day, Mike surprised him. "Hey, Sulley, there's something I want to show you."

It was Boo's reconstructed door, carefully glued back together. Sulley couldn't believe it. He cautiously opened the door. "Boo?"

"Kitty!"